MRS. MORTIFEE'S MOUSE

by
Linda Hendry

AN ALLIGATOR PRESS BOOK

HarperCollins*Publishers*Ltd

For Ratty

Mrs. Mortifee had a mouse in her house and she didn't like it one bit.

On Sunday the mouse was in

Mrs. Mortifee's teapot.

Mrs. Mortifee had coffee instead.

On Monday the mouse was in

Mrs. Mortifee's bowling ball.

Mrs. Mortifee decided to go jogging.

On Tuesday the mouse was in

Mrs. Mortifee's favorite shoes.

She had to wear her rubber boots.

On Wednesday

Mrs. Mortifee went shopping.

That afternoon

she built the perfect trap.

But on Thursday the mouse was in

Mrs. Mortifee's bathtub...

...And on Friday the mouse was in

Mrs. Mortifee's bed!

On Saturday

Mrs. Mortifee bought a cat.

She could hardly wait

to get home.

Now Mrs. Mortifee has
a mouse *and* a cat in her house...

...and she doesn't mind at all!